IT'S NOT MY FAULT!

Nancy Carlson

Carolrhoda Books, Inc./Minneapolis

Carolrhoda Books, Inc.
A division of Lerner Publishing Group
241 First Avenue North
Minneapolis, MN 55401 U.S.A.

Website address: www.lernerbooks.com

Library of Congress Cataloging-in-Publication Data

Carlson, Nancy L.
        It's not my fault! / written and illustrated by Nancy Carlson.
            p. cm.
        Summary: When he is called to the principal's office, George
    hurries to explain that other people were to blame for the many
    things that went wrong during the day, from his late arrival to the
    escape of some mice.
        ISBN: 1–57505–598–8 (lib. bdg. : alk. paper)
        [1. Responsibility—Fiction. 2. Schools—Fiction.] I. Title.
    PZ7.C21665 Iv 2003
    [E]—dc21   2002152916

Manufactured in the United States of America
    2 3 4 5 6 – JR – 08 07 06 05 04

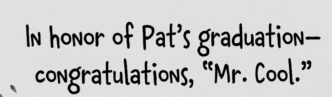

In honor of Pat's graduation—
congratulations, "Mr. Cool."

On Monday afternoon, George was called to Principal Flom's office.

"Come in, George," began Ms. Flom. "I'd like to . . ."

But before she could finish, George blurted out, "I can explain everything! I was late today, but **it's not my fault!**"

"I stayed up late last night to watch my favorite movie on TV.

I don't know what happened, but my alarm clock didn't work this morning and I overslept."

"I had to run in the halls to get to class on time.
That's when a kindergartner bumped into me.

My lunch spilled everywhere! I had to clean it up, and I was late to class."

"So it's all that kindergartner's fault I was late today."
"Well, George . . . ," said Ms. Flom.
"OK. I didn't get my math done either, but **it's not my fault!**

Because my lunch spilled all over the floor this morning, I didn't get to eat today."

"I was really hungry during gym class, and I had to sneak a candy bar.

Coach Ed caught me and told me to do fifty sit-ups!"

"Those sit-ups made me so tired, I couldn't pay attention in math class.

So it's all Coach Ed's fault I didn't get my math assignment done."

"Uh, George," said Ms. Flom.
"All right! I didn't catch these mice, but **it's not my fault!**

"It's not *my* fault I tripped.

But Mr. B. made me stay in during recess to clean up the paint."

"While I was trying to clean up the paint, that cage got in my way and fell over."

"Boy, do mice run fast when they get loose! I was trying to catch them when I was called to your office."

"So it's all *your* fault I didn't get to catch these mice...?"

"George!" exclaimed Ms. Flom. "I actually called you into my office to ask you to be on the school patrol."

"But it's not *my* fault you won't have time to discuss that today! You'll be busy staying after school to finish your math, clean up that paint, and . . .

When George finally got home, his mother said, "YOU'RE LATE!"

"I can explain," mumbled George. "Ms. Flom made me stay after school to finish my math, clean up paint, catch mice, and it's all my fault."
"Why is that?" asked his mother.